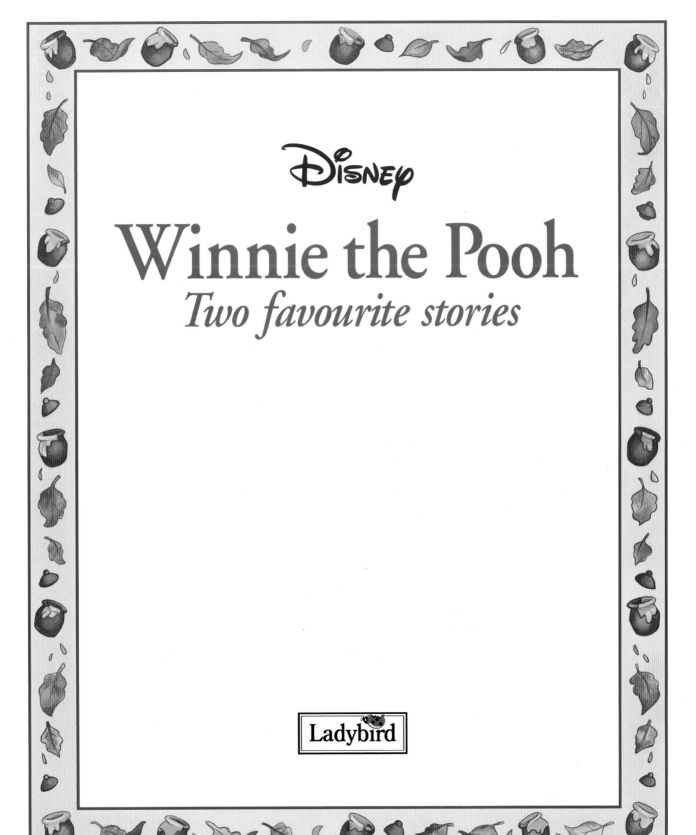

Disney

Winnie the Pooh
Two favourite stories

Ladybird

A catalogue record for this book is available from the British Library

Published by Ladybird Books Ltd
A subsidiary of the Penguin Group
A Pearson Company
LADYBIRD and the device of a Ladybird are trademarks of Ladybird Books Ltd Loughborough Leicestershire UK
© Disney MCMXCV
Based on the Pooh stories by A A Milne (copyright The Pooh Properties Trust)

Winnie the Pooh
and the honey tree

One sunny morning, in a little house somewhere deep in the Hundred Acre Wood, a very round bear named Winnie the Pooh was doing his stoutness exercises. He was just touching his toes when he felt his tummy rumble.

"Oh, my!" said Pooh. "This exercising is making me hungry – time for something to eat!" Pooh began to sing, "I'm short, fat and proud of that…" and danced towards the cupboard where he kept all his food.

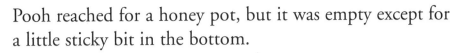

Pooh reached for a honey pot, but it was empty except for a little sticky bit in the bottom.

As he stuck his head in the pot to lick up the sticky bit, Pooh heard a buzzing noise. "A bee!" he cried, pulling his head out. "And bees mean honey for me to eat!"

So Pooh began to follow the bee through the Hundred Acre Wood, until he came to a very tall tree. Looking up, he saw lots of bees buzzing round a hole.

"Honey!" cried Pooh, greedily. He began to climb – up and up, to a branch right next to the hole. Inside, Pooh saw honey – *lots* of honey.

But as he leaned forward and put out his paw, the branch began to bend – *SNAP!* The branch broke and

down

went

Pooh...

...bouncing from branch to branch...

...until he ran out of branches...

…and landed headfirst in a prickly bush!

"Oh, bother!" said Pooh, rubbing his sore head. "It all comes, I suppose, from liking honey so much!"

Winnie the Pooh crawled out of the bush, brushed the prickles from his nose and began to think. And at last he came up with an idea…

First, he borrowed a big, blue balloon from his friend, Christopher Robin. "But you can't get honey with a balloon," Christopher Robin told Pooh.

"I can," said Pooh. "I shall hang onto the string and float up to the bee hole," he explained.

Then, Pooh rolled himself in some mud until he was covered from his nose to his toes.

"I'm pretending to be a little black rain cloud," Pooh told Christopher Robin, "to fool the bees."

"Silly old bear," said Christopher Robin as he watched Pooh float up, up, up into the sky.

Soon, Pooh Bear was dangling right outside the bee hole. He reached into the hole and pulled out a pawful of golden honey. But the bees began buzzing suspiciously around Pooh's head.

"Christopher Robin!" called Pooh, swatting at the bees and swinging wildly from the end of the balloon string. "I think the bees s-u-s-p-e-c-t that I am not a little black rain cloud!"

Suddenly, the knot in the string came undone and all the air rushed out of the balloon. Down fell Pooh, landing right on top of Christopher Robin!

"Oh, bother," said Pooh, shaking his head. "It all comes, I suppose, from liking honey so much!"

Now, Winnie the Pooh is not the sort of bear to give up easily so he decided to go and see Rabbit, who always had some honey in his house…

"How about a spot of lunch?" asked Rabbit. "Would you like condensed milk or honey on your bread?"

"Both," said Pooh, "but never mind the bread, thank you," he added, politely.

So Pooh ate and ate and ate. At last he said in a rather sticky voice, "I must be going now. Goodbye, Rabbit." And he began to climb slowly out of Rabbit's front door.

But just when Pooh's head had reached the outside and his feet were still dangling inside, his middle got stuck in the middle! Pooh tried to get out. Then he tried to get back in. But he couldn't do either!

"Oh, bother!" said Pooh. "It all comes from not having front doors big enough!"

"Nonsense!" said Rabbit, sharply. "It all comes from eating too much!" And off Rabbit went, hurrying out of his back door to fetch Christopher Robin.

Now there was nothing for Pooh to do but wait. Owl swooped down from his branch to talk to him.

"Pooh," he said, "you are definitely stuck. You are a wedged bear in a great tightness!"

After what seemed like a very long time, Rabbit came back with Christopher Robin. "Silly old bear!" he said.

Then he and Rabbit pulled and pulled and pulled.

But Pooh was still stuck tight!

At last, Christopher Robin said, "We're just going to have to wait for you to get thin enough to slide out."

So they waited…

…Christopher Robin read stories to Pooh…

…Owl lectured Pooh on the dangers of eating too much…

...Kanga brought Pooh a scarf to protect his head from the sun...

...and Eeyore made gloomy predictions about how long it might take for Pooh to get thinner. "It could be days," he said with a sigh. "Maybe weeks, even months," he added, shaking his head.

After some more time had passed, Rabbit grew tired of seeing Pooh's bottom and legs where his front door used to be. He decided to turn Pooh into something better to look at…

He wedged a picture frame around Pooh's middle, added two branches that looked like antlers and painted a face on Pooh's bottom.

For a finishing touch, Rabbit found a board and put it across Pooh's legs like a shelf. "That's more like it!" said Rabbit.

20

But then Kanga and Roo gave Pooh a bunch of flowers. And as Pooh sniffed the flowers, his nose started to tickle and his back end started to wriggle.

"Ah, ah, ah..." said Pooh. "...*CHOO!*"

Inside Rabbit's hole, Pooh kicked his legs and down came Rabbit's new shelf, antlers and all.

"Oh, no! Oh, dear!" said Rabbit, crossly. "Why did I ever invite that bear to lunch?"

That night, Rabbit heard voices outside his front door. He couldn't believe his ears—Pooh was asking Gopher for some honey!

"No! No! No!" Rabbit cried, rushing outside and snatching the honey pot from Pooh's paws.

Then he made a sign and stuck it right in front of Pooh. It read: DON'T FEED THE BEAR!

Next morning, Rabbit leaned against Pooh's bottom to rest – and Pooh moved! Rabbit cried out with delight. Then he hurried off as fast as he could to get Christopher Robin.

And Pooh's friends all came along to help as well. Rabbit began to push from behind. At the front, Christopher Robin grabbed Pooh's paws and began to pull. Kanga grabbed Christopher Robin, Eeyore grabbed Kanga and Roo grabbed Eeyore. "Heave-ho!" they cried, pulling as hard as they possibly could.

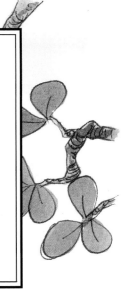

POP!

Pooh flew out of the doorway like a cork from a bottle and whizzed across the grass in front of Rabbit's house – straight towards another honey tree! He landed headfirst right inside a hole in the tree.

BUZZZZ! Pooh's sudden appearance startled the bees and they flew out of the tree and away over the treetops.

"We'll rescue you, Pooh!" called Christopher Robin.

But Pooh didn't want to be rescued. "Take your time!" he said happily, between large pawfuls of honey!

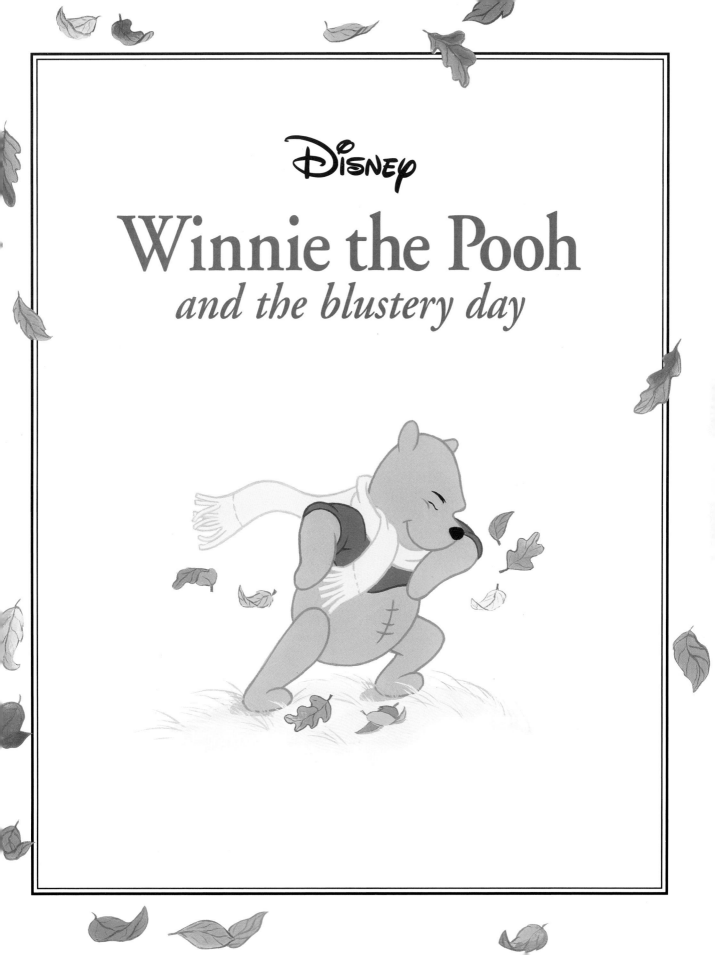

Winnie the Pooh
and the blustery day

On one particularly blustery day in the Hundred Acre Wood, Winnie the Pooh decided to visit his Thoughtful Spot. As he walked along, he made up a little hum. This is how it went:

"*Hum, dum, dum.*
Oh, the wind is lashing lustily,
And the leaves are rustling gustily.
So I think it's safe to say
It looks like a rather blustery day!"

Fortunately, Pooh Bear's Thoughtful Spot was in a sheltered place. He sat down on an old tree trunk and tried hard to think of something.

"Think, think, think, think, think," Pooh mumbled to himself. But nothing came to mind.

"Think, think, think," Pooh tried again, putting one paw to his head as if to catch any stray thoughts that might come wandering along.

Suddenly, Gopher popped out of his gopher hole and said, "Say, what's wrong, sonny? Got yourself a headache?"

"No," Pooh replied. "I was just thinking."

"Is that so?" said Gopher. "Well, if I were you, I'd think about skedaddling out of here. It's Windsday, you know."

"Windsday? Oh, so it is," said Pooh. And then he finally had a thought—and it was a good one at that. "I think I shall go and wish everyone a happy Windsday," Pooh announced. "And I shall begin with my very dear friend Piglet."

Now, Piglet lived in a very grand house in the middle of a beech tree. And on this blustery day, he was sweeping the fallen leaves away from his front door. He had just swept the last leaf away when a big gust of wind blew it right back at him, scooping him up and whisking him into the air.

"Happy Windsday, Piglet!" cried Pooh, running after him. "Where are you going?"

"That's what I'm asking myself," said Piglet. "Where?"

"And what do you think you will answer yourself?" Pooh asked, grabbing hold of Piglet's scarf just before he floated out of reach.

But Piglet didn't have time to answer Pooh's question – his scarf was unravelling! Like a pink kite on a long green string, Piglet went soaring off into the sky.

"Oh, dear! Oh, dear!" cried Piglet.

"Hold on tight, Piglet!" cried Pooh from down below.

Not far away, Rabbit was in his garden.

"Ah, what a refreshing day for harvesting," Rabbit said aloud, as he pulled up a large carrot.

Looking up, he suddenly saw Pooh heading towards him at top speed.

"Oh, no!" shouted Rabbit, waving his arms frantically.

"Happy Windsday," Pooh called, ploughing up a whole row of carrots.

"Oh, yes!" Rabbit chuckled as the juicy, ripe carrots fell straight into his wheelbarrow. "Next time I hope he ploughs right through my potato patch!"

The wind blew stronger and stronger. And before long, Piglet found himself blown right up against Owl's window.

Owl was woken from a peaceful snooze by the loud crash. "Whoo?" he called, opening his big round eyes. "Who is it?"

"It's me," Piglet said. "P-p-p-please, may I come in?"

"Well, I say now," Owl exclaimed, his eyes rounder than ever. "Someone has stuck Piglet onto my window."

Just then, Pooh's face appeared beside Piglet's, so Owl invited them in.

Soon, Pooh and Piglet were seated in Owl's cosy living room. "Am I correct in assuming that it is a rather blustery day outside?" asked Owl.

"Oh, yes! That reminds me," cried Pooh. "Happy Windsday, Owl."

"Windsday?" Owl hooted. "But it's just a mild breeze. It reminds me of the year my Aunt Clara went to visit her cousin…"

"Good," said Owl, settling back in his rocking chair. "That will just give me time to tell you about my Uncle Clyde…"

And that's just what Owl did. On and on and on he talked, until the blustery day turned into a blustery night.

For Pooh, when he was tucked up in bed, it turned out to be an anxious sort of night, filled with anxious sorts of noises. And one of the noises was a sound that had never been heard in the Hundred Acre Wood before:

"RRRRRRR!"

It wasn't a rumble. It wasn't a grumble. And it wasn't exactly a growl. But whatever it was, it was coming from just outside Pooh's door.

"Is that you, Piglet?" Pooh called, but no one answered. "Eeyore?" Pooh tried again. And finally, "Come in, Christopher Robin!"

When there was still no answer, Pooh got out of bed and went to investigate. And being a bear of very little brain, he decided to invite the new sound in.

"Hello, out there," he said, flinging his front door open.

Suddenly, a big, bouncy creature bounded in and knocked Pooh flat.

"RRRRRRR! Hello!" the creature said from on top of Pooh's chest.
"I'm Tigger."

"Oh," Pooh replied, looking up. "You scared me."

"Of course I did," Tigger said, good-naturedly. "Everyone's scared of
Tiggers. Who are you?"

"I'm Pooh," said Pooh.

"Glad to meet you," said Tigger. And with no further ado, he climbed off Pooh and stuck out both of his paws. "Tigger's my name. T-I-double Guh-Er. That spells Tigger!"

"But what is a Tigger?" Pooh asked, puzzled.

"Tiggers are wonderful things," Tigger replied proudly, as he began to bounce around the room. "They're bouncy, trouncy, pouncy," he sang, "but the most wonderful thing about Tiggers is – I'm the only one!"

And with that, he went bouncing out of the door and into the night.

Now, the very blustery night turned into a very rainy night. Pooh went back to sleep and had terrible dreams about all sorts of strange creatures who were trying to steal his honey. Then one of them turned into a watering can and began sprinkling him with water!

Pooh woke up with a start, and the strange creatures had gone. But the water hadn't, it was still there. It was already up to Pooh's knees, and more was dripping through the ceiling. He waded across the floor to his mirror and stared thoughtfully at the very damp bear reflected there.

"Is it raining in there?" Pooh asked the reflection.

As a matter of fact, Pooh wasn't the only one feeling damp, for it was raining all over the Hundred Acre Wood. The rain came down, down, down, and the river rose up, up, up, rising so high that it finally flowed into Piglet's house.

Poor Piglet was terrified. With the water swirling around him, he grabbed a pen and some paper and frantically scribbled a note:

HELP! P-P-PIGLET. (ME.)

Then, he put the message into a bottle and threw it out of his window into the raging river.

As the rain continued to come down, down, down, Piglet tried to scoop it up into a big iron pot. But the pot was not—most definitely not—big enough for all the water!

Floating on top of a wooden chair, Piglet kept on bailing, and he was so busy bailing that he didn't notice as he went sailing through the open door.

Meanwhile, Pooh was having quite a difficult time himself. He had managed to save ten honey pots, and was sitting with them on the branch of a tree, high above the river. More than ready for his breakfast, he stuck his head into one of the pots. But as Pooh tried to scoop up his breakfast, the river scooped up Pooh, for he fell off the branch and into the swirling water below. Upside down, with his head still stuck in the honey pot, Pooh was carried along with the water's current.

The water hadn't reached Christopher Robin's house, so that's where everyone was gathering. Everyone except Piglet, Pooh and Eeyore, that is. Eeyore was still hunting for a new home for Owl.

Then someone found the bottle with Piglet's message in it. Christopher Robin lost no time. He turned to Owl and said, "You must fly to Piglet's house and tell him we will rescue him."

Owl soon found Piglet—and Pooh! "A rescue is being planned," Owl said. "Be brave."

"It's awfully hard to be b-b-brave when you're such a s-s-small animal," Piglet pointed out.

"Then to divert your small mind from your unfortunate predicament, I shall tell you an amusing anecdote," Owl offered. "It concerns a distant cousin of mine…"

Owl had just begun his story when Piglet cried, "I beg your pardon, Owl, but I think we're coming to a flutterfall, a falatterfall, a very big w-waterfall!"

"Please," said Owl, holding up a warning wing. "No interruptions."

But Piglet was already being carried away by the current. A moment later he fell over the waterfall, with Pooh, still stuck in the honey pot, close behind him.

Head over heels the two friends tumbled down the rushing, gushing waterfall – down, down, down they went until they finally landed in a quiet pool far, far below.

"Oh, there you are, Pooh Bear," Owl said as Pooh popped up on Piglet's chair. "Now, to continue my story…"

Fortunately for Pooh, Owl didn't have time to finish his story, for they quickly floated to the river's edge where Christopher Robin and the others were waiting.

"Look everyone, there's Pooh!" Christopher Robin cried, lifting him gently off the chair. "Pooh Bear, thank goodness you're safe. But where is Piglet?"

All of a sudden something popped up from under the chair. It was Pooh's honey pot!

"H-h-here I am," Piglet replied from inside the pot.

"Pooh!" Christopher Robin cried again. "You rescued Piglet!"

"I did?" Pooh said.

"Yes," Christopher Robin said, patting Pooh on the head. "And it was a very brave thing to do. You are a hero!"

"I am?" Pooh asked.

"Yes," said Christopher Robin. "And as soon as the flood is over, I shall give you a hero party."

Just then, Eeyore came trudging along. "I found a house for Owl," he said.

"Good show!" Owl hooted, happily. "Where is it?"

"Follow me and I'll show you," said Eeyore.

So everyone followed Eeyore. But much to their surprise, when they got to Owl's new house, it turned out to be – Piglet's house!

"This is Owl's new house," Eeyore said, proudly. "What do you think of it?"

There was a moment of silence.

"Tell them it's your house, Piglet," Pooh whispered to his friend.

But Piglet didn't have the heart to disappoint Owl. "No," he sniffed. "This house belongs to our very good friend, Owl."

"But Piglet," Rabbit said, "where will *you* live?"

"With me," Pooh broke in, taking Piglet's hand in his. "You will live with me, won't you, Piglet?"

"With you?" Piglet said, wiping a tear from his eye. "Oh, thank you, Pooh Bear. Of course I will."

"Piglet, that was a very grand thing to do," Christopher Robin said, taking Piglet's other hand.

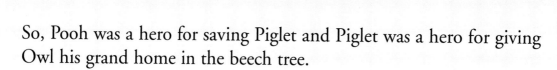

So, Pooh was a hero for saving Piglet and Piglet was a hero for giving Owl his grand home in the beech tree.

Suddenly, Pooh Bear had his second good thought in as many days. "Christopher Robin," he said, "can we make a one-hero party into a two-hero party?"

"Of course we can," said Christopher Robin. "Silly old bear!"

And that's exactly what they did!